MARVEL

THOR

pi kids®

Phoenix International Publications, Inc.

Chicago • London • New York • Hamburg • Mexico City • Paris • Sydney

Odin, father of Thor, has made a special gift for his son. But the mighty hammer Mjölnir may be lifted only by one who is worthy. After years of trials, Thor is ready. The people of Asgard gather to see him claim his gift and become Thor, Prince of Asgard!

As Thor lifts Mjölnir for the first time, find these excited Asgardians in the crowd:

Heimdall watches the Bifrost, which connects Asgard to other realms. The all-seeing guardian looks for any signs of danger in the cosmos. He notices something strange on Midgard—*Earth*, to humans—and alerts Thor. Worried about his mortal friends, the Son of Odin investigates.

As Thor makes his way, stand with Heimdall and gaze at these shapes in the stars:

"T" of Thor

Mjölnir

Steed of the Bifrost

Great Frog

Thor's Helmet

Heimdall's Blade

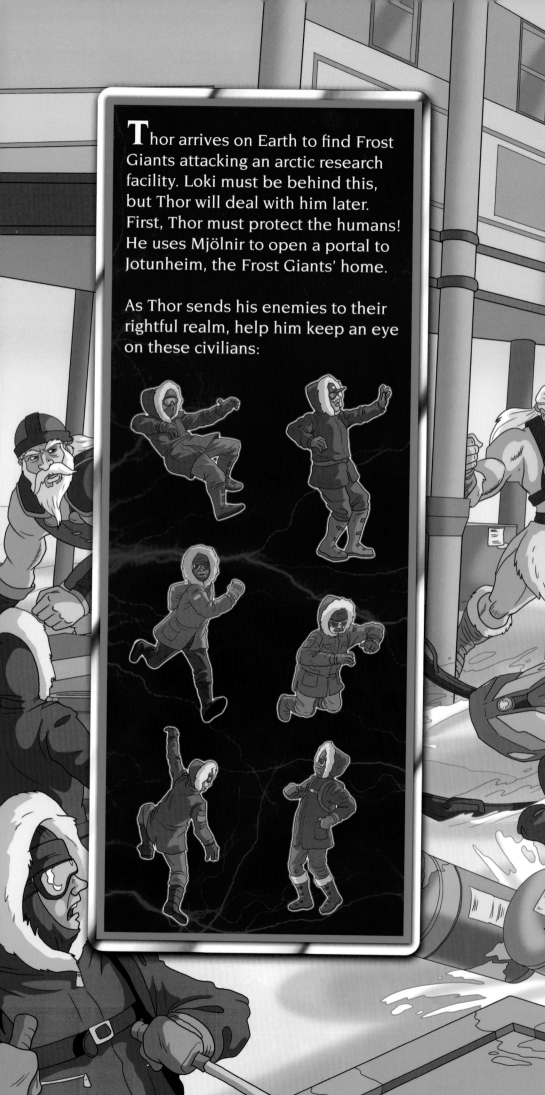

Thor arrives on Earth to find Frost Giants attacking an arctic research facility. Loki must be behind this, but Thor will deal with him later. First, Thor must protect the humans! He uses Mjölnir to open a portal to Jotunheim, the Frost Giants' home.

As Thor sends his enemies to their rightful realm, help him keep an eye on these civilians:

After dispatching the Frost Giants, Thor prepares to track down Loki. Just before he takes off, he receives the call: "Avengers assemble!" Like lightning from a cumulonimbus cloud, the Mighty Avenger blasts to his friends' aid.

As Thor approaches Avengers Tower, stay vigilant by locating these Hydra spies:

Hydra agents are everywhere! Worried citizens watch the news as the Avengers and Thor battle with the evil organization. Will the heroes manage to stop Hydra again? Even die-hard Avengers fans are concerned about the outcome.

Cheer on the heroes by spotting these collectibles:

Hawkeye's arrow

Avengers watch

Avengers necktie

Mjölnir paperweight

wearable Iron Man helmet

replica of Thor's helmet

Thor action figure

Cap's collectible shield

With Hydra defeated, Thor sets his sights on Loki again. But while Thor was busy, his adoptive brother was finishing his slipperiest spell yet. When Thor arrives to confront Loki, the trickster turns Thor into a frog!

While Thor figures out how to turn back from green to blond, look out for these new perils:

mousetrap

this boot

heron

this rat

sewer alligator

this cat

Thor regains his true form with the help of his friend Doctor Strange, but he's still hopping mad! Loki flees to prepare one last deception. He hides in a carnival house of mirrors and projects multiple Lokis around the room. When Thor arrives, he knows not where to strike!

Luckily, Doctor Strange sees through the deception. Help him point out these impostors:

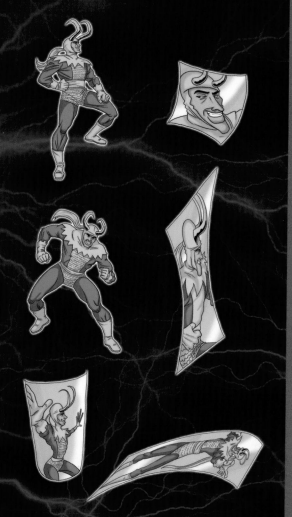

With Loki defeated, Thor triumphantly returns to Asgard. Odin throws a feast in celebration, and he even invites Thor's mortal friends to attend. Mjölnir is in good hands, indeed.

No one knows how to feast like an Asgardian! Take part by tasting these delicacies:

Thor's thundersticks

this loaf of bread

this stuffed fowl

Odin's special sauce

these éclairs

cosmic cordial

Asgardian salad

Thor knows that even one worthy of wielding Mjölnir needs the help of friends and family to be a true hero. Head back to the halls of Asgard, and look for these important allies:

The Warriors Three

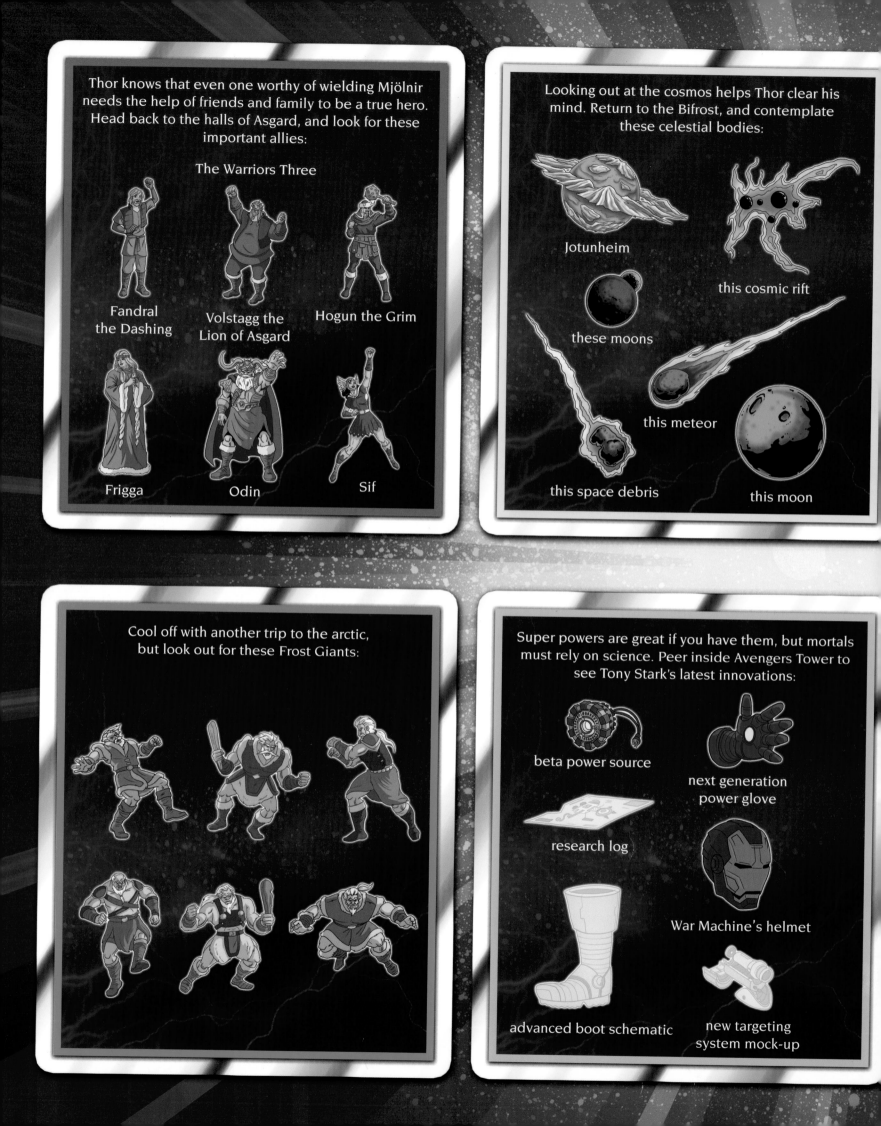

Fandral the Dashing

Volstagg the Lion of Asgard

Hogun the Grim

Frigga

Odin

Sif

Looking out at the cosmos helps Thor clear his mind. Return to the Bifrost, and contemplate these celestial bodies:

Jotunheim

this cosmic rift

these moons

this meteor

this space debris

this moon

Cool off with another trip to the arctic, but look out for these Frost Giants:

Super powers are great if you have them, but mortals must rely on science. Peer inside Avengers Tower to see Tony Stark's latest innovations:

beta power source

next generation power glove

research log

War Machine's helmet

advanced boot schematic

new targeting system mock-up

Take a break from the news to look back at the living room shelves for these bits of bric-a-brac:

hanging hearts flowerpot

stuffed jackalope

Mickey plush

hula doll

grinning gnome

cross-eyed cuckoo clock

cool flamingo

floral teapot

Frogs feast, too. Assume the form again and find these tasty frog delicacies:

It's nice to reflect after a long journey. Go back to the house of mirrors and find more multiplied items:

Thor loves to regale listeners with tales of his feats. Return to the great feast and find these souvenirs he's collected over the course of his journey:

arctic ice

scientist's goggles

Tony Stark's glove

funhouse reflection

frog

Avengers mug